red hat

red hat

by LITA JUDGE

SCHOLASTIC INC.

For Uma

ISBN 978-0-545-68699-0

Copyright © 2013 by Lita Judge. All rights reserved. Published by
Scholastic Inc., 557 Broadway, New York, NY 10012, by arrangement with
Atheneum Books for Young Readers, an imprint of Simon & Schuster Children's Publishing Division.
SCHOLASTIC and associated logos are trademarks and/or registered trademarks of Scholastic Inc.

12 11 10 9 8 7 6 5 4 3 2 1   14 15 16 17 18 19/0

Printed in the U.S.A.   40

First Scholastic printing, January 2014

Book design by Ann Bobco
The text for this book is set in Fairfield LH and Bodoni Oldface.
The illustrations for this book are rendered in pencil and watercolor.

Swish swash swish swash

ROWeeeeee

shwooop

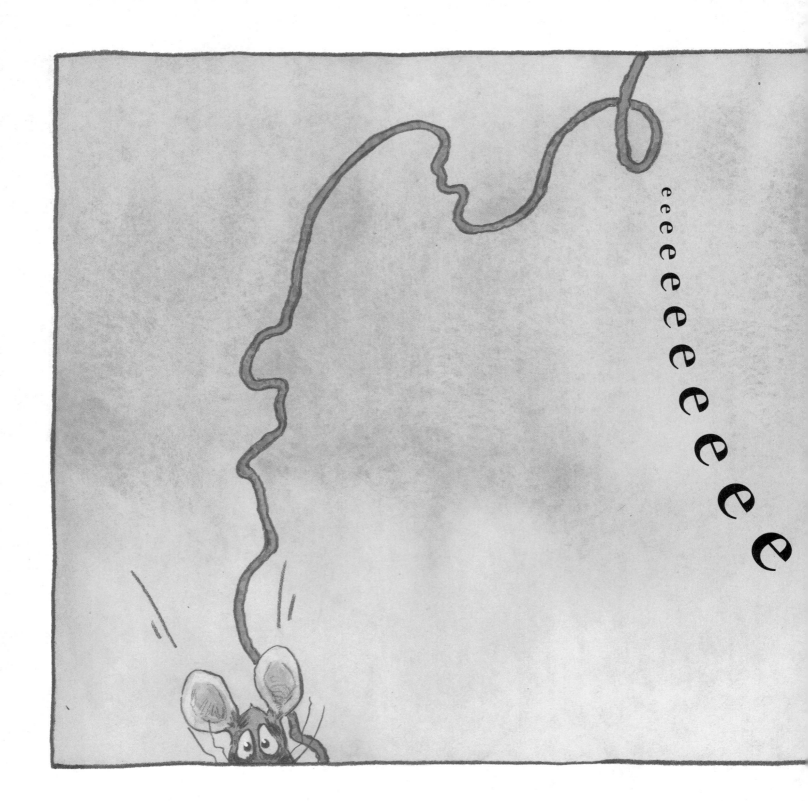

eep

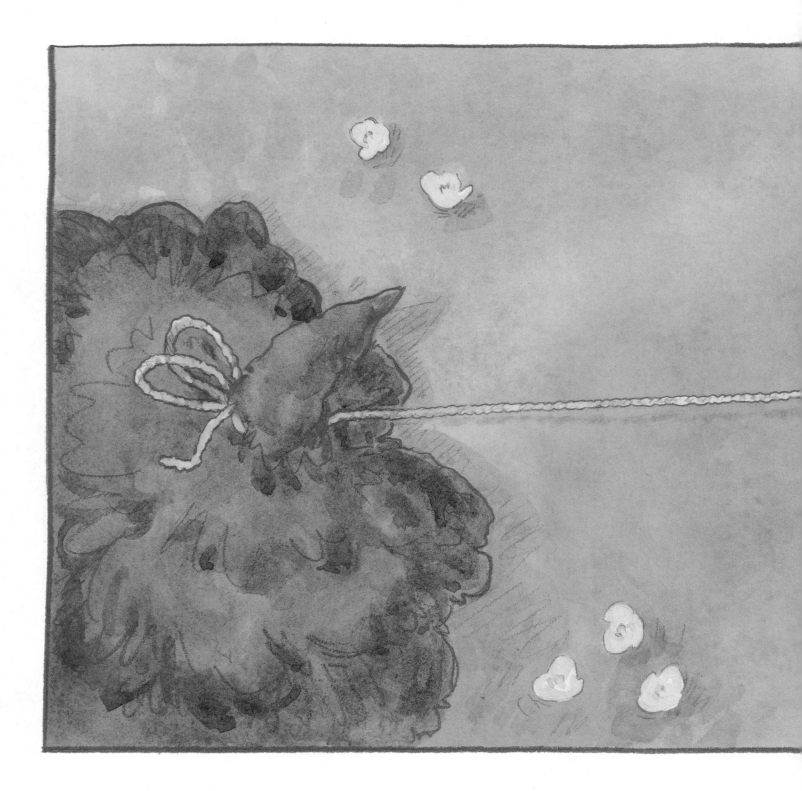

Tink-a-tink
tink

The End

LITA JUDGE is the award-winning author and illustrator of several children's books, including *Red Sled*, *One Thousand Tracings*, and *Pennies for Elephants*. She lives with her husband and cats in the New Hampshire woods, watching animals and dreaming up stories. You can visit her online at litajudge.com.

Author photograph by Dave Judge